Paddington

Something Nasty in the Kitchen

written by *Michael Bond*
illustrated by *John Lobban*

Young Lions
An Imprint of HarperCollinsPublishers

First published in Great Britain 1992 in Young Lions

Young Lions is an imprint of the Children's Division,
part of HarperCollins Publishers Ltd,
77/85 Fulham Palace Road, Hammersmith,
London W6 8JB

Text copyright © Michael Bond 1991
Illustrations copyright © John Lobban 1991

Adapted from *Something Nasty in the Kitchen* from
Paddington Helps Out, text copyright © Michael Bond 1960.
Available in Young Lions.

The author asserts the moral right to be
identified as the author of this work.

ISBN 0 00 674311 0

Printed and bound in Great Britain by
HarperCollins Book Manufacturing, Glasgow

Part One

"Two days!" exclaimed Mrs Brown, staring at Dr MacAndrew in horror. "Do you mean to say we've to stay in bed for two whole days?"

"Aye," said Dr MacAndrew, "there's a nasty wee bug going the rounds and if ye don't I'll no be responsible for the consequences."

"But Mrs Bird's away until tomorrow," said Mrs Brown. "And so are Jonathan and Judy ... and ... and that only leaves Paddington."

Dr MacAndrew snapped his bag shut. "Two days and not a moment less."
He paused at the door with a twinkle in his eye.

Whatever happens you'll no die of starvation. Yon wee bears verra fond of his inside!

Then he went downstairs to tell Paddington the news.

Oh dear, I think I feel worse already.

Part Two

Paddington felt most important as he listened to what Doctor MacAndrew had to say.

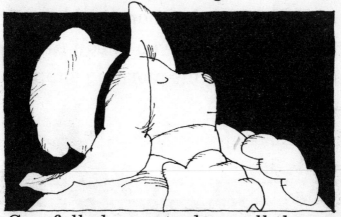

Carefully he wrote down all the instructions.
After the doctor had left, Paddington hurried back into the kitchen to collect his shopping basket on wheels.

Usually with Paddington,
shopping in the market was a very
leisurely affair. He liked to stop
and have a chat with the various
traders in the Portobello Road. But
on this particular morning he
hardly had time even to call in at
the bakers for his morning supply
of buns.

It was early and Mr Gruber hadn't
yet opened his shutters,

so Paddington wrapped one of the
hot buns in a piece of paper,

wrote a message on the outside
saying who it was from and
explained that he wouldn't be
along for elevenses that morning,

won't
see you this
morning.

and pushed it through the
letter-box.

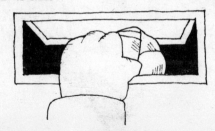

He finished the shopping and went
to the chemist with Doctor
MacAndrew's prescription,

then Paddington made his way
quickly home to number thirty-two
Windsor Gardens.

It wasn't often Paddington had the chance to lend a paw around the house, let alone cook the dinner, and he was looking forward to it.

In particular, there was a new duster of Mrs Bird's he'd had his eye on for several days which he was very anxious to test.

He disappeared into the kitchen.

"They are rather thick," agreed Mrs Brown, looking at one doubtfully. "He said they were emergency ones. I'm not sure what he meant by that. I do hope nothing's wrong."

"I don't like the sound of it," said Mr Brown. "There've been several nasty silences this morning— as if something was going on." He sniffed. "And there seems to be a strong smell of burnt feathers coming from somewhere."

"Well you'd better eat them, Henry," warned Mrs Brown. "He's used some of his special marmalade and I'm sure they're meant to be a treat."

"Yes, but _six!_" grumbled Mr Brown. "I'm not even very keen on marmalade. And at twelve o'clock in the morning! I shan't want any lunch."

He looked
thoughtfully at the
window and then at
the plate of
sandwiches again.

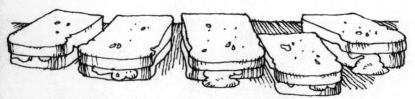

"No, Henry," said Mrs Brown,
reading his thoughts. "You're not
giving any to the birds. I don't
suppose they like marmalade.
Anyway," she added, "Paddington
did say something about lunch
being late, so you may be glad of
them."

"If you ask me," said Mr Brown, "you're probably much better off being in the dark." He took a long drink from his cup then jumped up in bed spluttering.

Henry dear, do be careful. You'll have coffee all over the sheets.

coffee!

did you say this was coffee?

"_I_ didn't, dear," said Mrs Brown mildly. "Paddington did." She took a sip from her own cup and then made a wry face. "It has got a rather unusual taste."

Unusual! It tastes like nothing on earth. It's got some funny green things floating in it too!

"Have a marmalade sandwich,"
said Mrs Brown. "It'll help to take
the taste away."

Mr Brown gave
his wife an
expressive look.
"Two days!" he
said, sinking
back into bed.
"Two whole days!"

Part Three

Downstairs, Paddington was in a bit of a mess. So, for that matter was the kitchen, the hall, the dining room and the stairs.

Things hadn't really gone right since he'd lifted up a corner of the dining room carpet in order to sweep some dust underneath and had discovered a number of very interesting old newspapers.

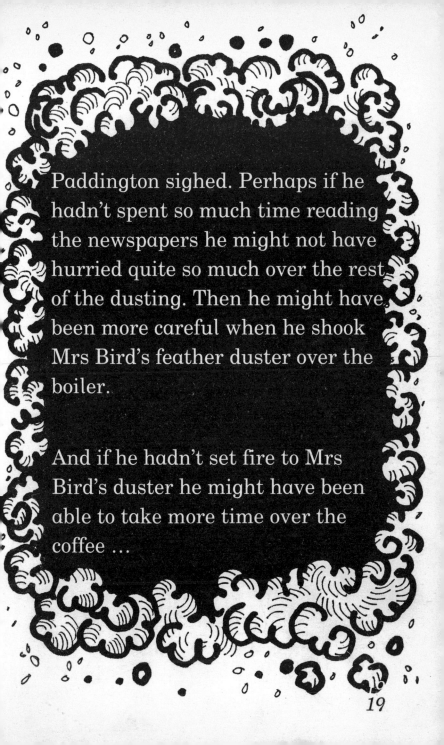

Paddington sighed. Perhaps if he hadn't spent so much time reading the newspapers he might not have hurried quite so much over the rest of the dusting. Then he might have been more careful when he shook Mrs Bird's feather duster over the boiler.

And if he hadn't set fire to Mrs Bird's duster he might have been able to take more time over the coffee …

Quite early in the morning
Paddington had run out of
saucepans. It was the first big
meal he had ever cooked and he
wanted it to be something special.
He consulted Mrs Bird's cookery
book, then he'd drawn out a special
menu in red ink with a bit of
everything in it.

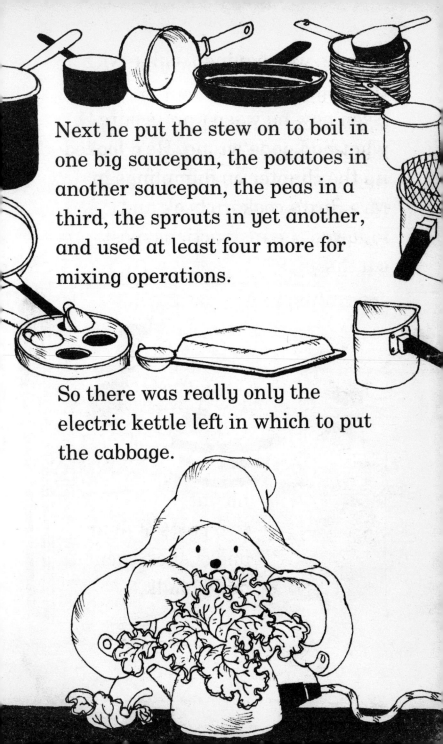

Next he put the stew on to boil in one big saucepan, the potatoes in another saucepan, the peas in a third, the sprouts in yet another, and used at least four more for mixing operations.

So there was really only the electric kettle left in which to put the cabbage.

Now he was having trouble with the dumplings!

Even now he wasn't quite sure what had gone wrong. He'd looked up the chapter on dumplings in Mrs Bird's cookery book and followed the instructions most carefully:

he put
two parts of flour
one of suet, then
added milk,

before stirring the whole lot
together.

But somehow, instead of the mixture turning into neat balls as it showed in the picture, it had all gone runny.

Then when he'd added more flour and suet, it had gone lumpy instead and stuck to his fur, so that he'd had to add more milk and then more flour and suet, until he had a huge mountain of dumpling mixture in the middle of the kitchen table.

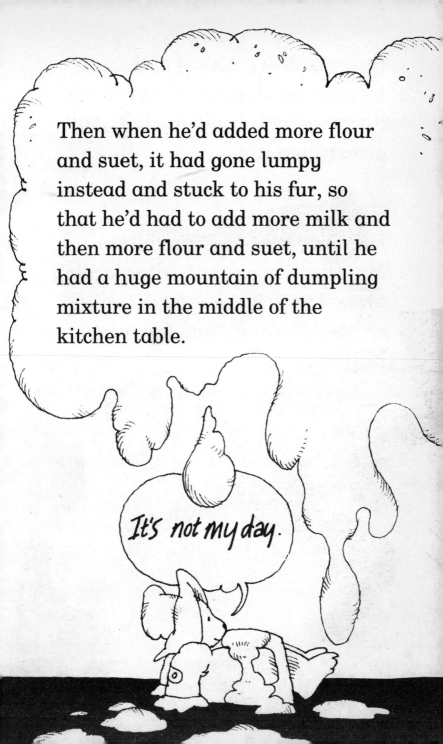

It's not my day.

He wiped his paws carefully on Mrs Bird's apron and, after looking around for a large enough bowl, scraped the dumpling mixture into his hat.

It was a lot heavier than he had expected and he had a job lifting it up onto the stove. It was even more difficult putting the mixture into the stew, as it kept sticking to his paws – and as fast as he
got it off one paw,
it stuck to the other.

In the end he had to sit on the draining board and use the broom handle.

Paddington wasn't very impressed with Mrs Bird's cookery book. The instructions seemed all wrong. Not only had the dumplings been difficult to make, but the ones they showed in the picture were much too small. They weren't a bit like the ones Mrs Bird usually served. Even Paddington rarely managed more than two of Mrs Bird's dumplings.

Paddington scraped the last of the
mixture off his paws and pushed
the saucepan lid down hard.

The steam from the saucepan had
made his fur go soggy and he sat in
the middle of the floor for several
minutes getting his breath back
and mopping his brow with an old
dishcloth.

As he sat scraping the remains of
the dumplings out of his hat and
licking the spoon, he felt
something move behind him ...

Not only that, but out of the corner of his eye he could see a shadow on the floor – which definitely hadn't been there a moment before.

Paddington sat very still, holding his breath and listening. It wasn't so much a noise as a feeling, and it seemed to be creeping nearer and nearer, making a soft swishing noise as it came. Paddington felt his fur beginning to stand on end.

There came the sound of

a slow

across the kitchen floor.

Just as he was summoning up
enough courage to look over his
shoulder,

there was a

from the direction of the stove.

Without waiting to see what it was
Paddington pulled his hat down
over his head and ran, slamming
the door behind him.

Part Four

Paddington arrived in the hall just
as there was a loud knock on the
front door.

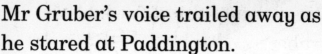

Mr Gruber's voice trailed away as he stared at Paddington.

Why Mr Brown, You're all white! Is anything the matter?

Don't worry Mr Gruber, It's only some of Mrs Bird's flour. I'm afraid I can't raise my hat because it's stuck down with dumpling mixture — but I'm very glad you've come because there's something nasty in the kitchen!

"What sort of thing?" asked Mr Gruber.

"I don't know, but it's got a shadow and it's making a funny noise," said Paddington.

Mr Gruber looked around nervously for something to defend himself with. "We'll soon see about that," he said, taking a warming pan off the wall.

Paddington led the way back to the kitchen and then stood to one side by the door.

"After you, Mr Gruber," he said politely.

He grasped the warming pan firmly in both hands and then kicked open the door.

"I don't think it's a *who*, Mr Gruber," said Paddington, peering round the door. "It's a *what!*"

"Good heavens!" exclaimed Mr Gruber, staring at the sight which met his eyes. "What has been going on?"

Over most of the kitchen there was a thin film of flour. There was flour on the table, in the sink, on the floor: in fact over practically everything.

And something large and white
was hanging over the side of the
stove!

Mr Gruber stared at it for a
moment and then advanced
cautiously across the kitchen. He
poked it with the handle of the
warming pan.

There was a loud squelching noise.
Mr Gruber jumped back.

A part broke away
and fell with a
plop to the
floor.

"Good heavens!" he exclaimed again. "I do believe it's some kind of dumpling, Mr Brown. I've never seen quite such a big one before. No wonder it made you jump."

Mr Gruber lifted Paddington's old dumpling into the washing-up bowl.

No wonder yours were so big Mr Brown, you must have used almost a whole bag of flour!

"Two bags," said Paddington. "I don't know what Mrs Bird will say when she hears about it."

Mr Gruber staggered into the garden. "Perhaps, if we buy her some more, she won't mind quite so much."

Mr Gruber sniffed. "I m... all smells very nice. If we... some more dumplings quic... everything else should be ju... about ready."

As he handed Paddington the flour and suet, Mr Gruber explained how dumplings became very much larger when they were cooked and that it really needed only a small amount of mixture to make quite large ones.

Part Five

"That's strange," said Mr Brown, as he stared out of the bedroom window. "There's a big white thing suddenly appeared in the garden. Just behind the nasturtiums."

"Nonsense, Henry," said Mrs Brown. "You must be seeing things."

"I'm not," said Mr Brown, rubbing his glasses and taking another look. "It's all white and shapeless and it looks horrible. Mr Curry has seen it too – he's peering over the fence at it now. Do you know what it is, Paddington?"

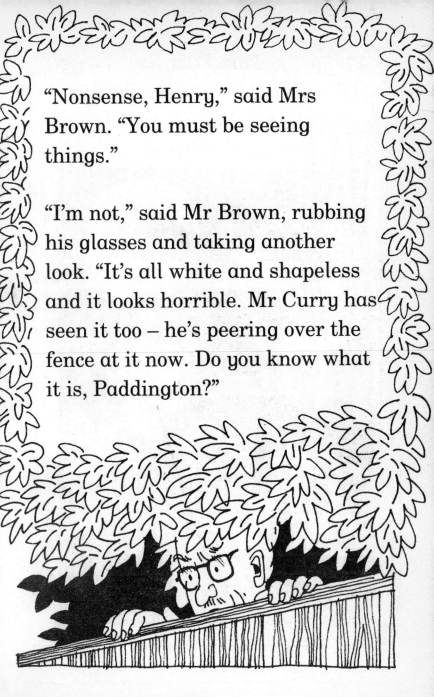

"A big white thing, Mr Brown?" said Paddington vaguely, joining him at the window.

"Henry," said Mrs Brown. "Do come away from there and decide what you're having for lunch. Paddington's gone to a lot of trouble writing out a menu for us."

Mr Brown took the menu and his face brightened as he studied it.

Menue
Soop
fish
ommlets
rowst beef
stew with dumplings
potatows
Brussle sprowts pees
Cabbage - Greyvy
Marmalade and Custard
Coffee

54

"How nice!" exclaimed
Mr Brown, when he had
finished reading it.
"And what a good idea
putting pieces of
vegetable on the side
as illustrations.
I've never seen that
done before."

"They're not really
meant to be
there, Mr Brown.
I'm afraid they
came off my paws.

"Well, you know, I rather fancy some soup and fish myself," said Mr Brown.

Mrs Brown drew him to one side.

"What's that, Mary?" asked Mr Brown, who was a bit slow to grasp things at times. "Oh! Oh, I see … er … on second thoughts, Paddington, I think perhaps I'll have the stew."

"That's good," said Paddington, "because I've got it on a tray outside all ready."

Paddington staggered in carrying first one plate and then another piled high with stew.

"I must say I didn't expect anything like this," said Mr Brown.

"Did you cook it all by yourself, Paddington?" asked Mrs Brown.

"Well...almost all," replied
Paddington truthfully. "I had a bit
of an accident with the dumplings
and so Mr Gruber helped me make
some more."

"You're sure you have enough for
your own lunch?" said Mrs Brown
anxiously.

Paddington thought about the
kitchen.

"Oh yes," he said. "There is enough
to last for days and days."

"Well, I think you should be congratulated," said Mr Brown. "I'm enjoying it to no end. I bet there aren't many bears who can say they've cooked a meal like this. It's fit for a queen."

Paddington's eyes lit up with pleasure as he listened to Mr and Mrs Brown.

It had been a lot of hard work but he was glad it had all been worthwhile – even if there was a lot of mess to clear up.

"You know, Henry," said Mrs Brown, as Paddington hurried off downstairs to see Mr Gruber. "We ought to think ourselves very lucky having a bear like Paddington about the house in an emergency."

Mr Brown lay back on his pillow
and surveyed the mountain of food
on his plate.